Terence Blacker writes  and adults. The best-s... first published in 1989 into 15 languages so ... children include The T........, The Angel Factory, Homebird and the Hotshots series. When he is not writing he likes to play the guitar, write songs and score goals for his football team.

What the reviewers have said about Ms Wiz:

"Hilarious and hysterical"
Susan Hill, Sunday Times

"Terence Blacker has created a splendid character in the magical Ms Wiz. Enormous fun"
The Scotsman

"Sparkling zany humour . . . brilliantly funny"
Children's Books of the Year

# IN CONTROL,
# MS WIZ?

# MS WIZ
# GOES LIVE

# MS WIZ –
# BANNED!

## Terence Blacker

*Illustrated by Tony Ross*

MACMILLAN
CHILDREN'S BOOKS

*In Control, Ms Wiz?*
First published 1990 by Piccadilly Press Ltd
Young Piper edition published 1990 by Pan Books
This edition published 1996 by Macmillan Children's Books
*Ms Wiz Goes Live*
First published 1990 by Piccadilly Press Ltd
Young Piper edition published 1991 by Pan Books
This edition published 1996 by Macmillan Children's Books
*Ms Wiz – Banned!*
First published 1990 by Piccadilly Press Ltd
Young Piper edition published 1991 by Pan Macmillan Children's Books
This edition published 1997 by Macmillan Children's Books

This omnibus edition published 2003 by Macmillan Children's Books
a division of Macmillan Publishers Limited
20 New Wharf Road, London N1 9RR
Basingstoke and Oxford
www.panmacmillan.com

Associated companies throughout the world

ISBN 0 330 42039 9

Text copyright © Terence Blacker 1990
Illustrations copyright © Tony Ross 1996, 1997

1 3 5 7 9 8 6 4 2

A CIP catalogue record for this book is available from
the British Library

Phototypeset by Intype London Ltd
Printed and bound in Great Britain by Mackays of Chatham plc, Kent

# In Control,
# Ms Wiz?

# CHAPTER ONE

# "Who was that woman?"

Above Mr Goff's desk at the Latimer Road Library was a sign which read "QUIET, PLEASE!" Today, as usual, it was being ignored.

In the children's corner, a group of five-year-olds were laughing at a story being read to them by their teacher.

By one of the armchairs, a blue-bottle was buzzing around the head of an old man who had fallen asleep.

Among the bookshelves, the new assistant librarian was flicking her duster at the books like a charioteer cracking a whip.

At the front desk, Mr Goff was sniffling into his handkerchief.

And, in the reference section, Peter

Harris – "Podge" to everyone who knew him – was telling his school friend Jack Beddows some really interesting facts he had just discovered.

"Did you know that in 1955, Phillip Yadzik of Chicago, USA, ate 77 large hamburgers in two hours?"

"Gross," said Jack, who was trying to read a football book.

"Or that the heaviest man in the

world came from East Ham, England, and weighed an astonishing 59 stone?"

"Mmm, big," said Jack.

"And that the world's largest jelly—"

"Podge," said Jack, putting down his book. "Did you know that the most annoying person in the entire universe is Podge 'Motormouth' Harris of London, England, who once

had a *Guinness Book of Records* pushed right up his left nostril because he talked about food all the time?"

"All right, all right," said Podge. "I was just trying to improve your general knowledge."

At that moment, the sniffling noise coming from Mr Goff's desk stopped. He took a deep breath and went, "Wah-wah-wah-WAAHHH!"

It was an extraordinary noise for anyone to make and it was particularly strange coming from Mr Goff, who was a timid, polite man. Normally, the only sound he ever made was the occasional "Sssshhh!"

Everybody stared. Mr Goff removed his spectacles and wiped them with a handkerchief. He looked around the library, sniffed a few times and took another deep breath.

"WAAAAHHHHHH!"

"Fire!" said the old man in the armchair, waking up with a start. "Don't panic! I heard the siren! Pensioners out first!"

"Podge," said Jack out of the side of his mouth. "I think the librarian is crying."

"How embarrassing," said Podge.

The teacher who had been reading to the children walked over to the front desk.

"Are you all right, Mr Goff?" she asked.

The librarian sniffed miserably.

"Perhaps it's hay fever," said the old man, who had now realized that the noise which had woken him was not a fire alarm.

Podge and Jack joined the group now standing around the front desk. They felt sorry for Mr Goff but, not being used to grown librarians

bursting into tears in the middle of
the day, they couldn't think of
anything to say.

The new assistant librarian, a
young woman with her dark hair in
a ponytail, went round to the other
side of the desk and put her arm
around Mr Goff.

"Cheer up," she said. "It might
never happen."

"It already has," said the librarian

6

miserably. He gave her the sheet of paper that he had been reading. "Look at this note from the council."

"*Notice of closure,*" the assistant librarian read out. "*The council gives notice that, as from the end of this month, the Latimer Road Library will be closed—*"

"Oh dear," said the teacher.

"*—and that all the books will be transferred to the nearby St Edward's Road Library—*"

"Nearby?" said the old man. "It's too far for me to walk to."

"*The library staff will be given jobs in another library. Signed, The Chief Leisure Officer.*"

"I don't want a job in another library," said Mr Goff, his voice cracking as if he were about to cry again. The teacher put her arm around his shoulders.

"There, there," she said.

"Jack," said Podge, looking closely at the assistant librarian, who was now taking off her nylon cleaning coat. "Does she remind you of someone?"

"Yes, she does," said Jack. "But what on earth is she doing here?"

The assistant librarian briskly peeled off the gloves in which she had been dusting the shelves. Standing there in her purple T-shirt and jeans, she looked quite different.

"It must be her," said Podge. "Who else would wear black nail varnish to work in a library?"

"That's enough talk," said the assistant librarian with her hands on her hips. "It's time for action. The end of the month – that means they'll be closing the library on Friday, unless we can stop them. Jack, Podge – I'll need your help. Now here's what we're going to do . . ."

Jack and Podge exchanged glances. She knew their names. "Here we go again," said Podge with a smile.

A few minutes later, the assistant librarian gathered up her belongings and strode out of the library, saying she had some spells to prepare.

"Spells?" said the teacher after she had left. "What's going on?"

"Yes, who *was* that woman in the purple T-shirt?" asked Mr Goff.

"That was Ms Wiz," said Podge.

"If anyone can save the library," said Jack, "Ms Wiz can. She has magic on her side."

"Good old Ms Wiz," said Mr Goff. He didn't seem convinced.

*

"Dad," said Podge that evening, as the Harris family ate dinner. "Is it true that the council wants to close the library?"

"It is," said Mr Harris, who was a councillor. "There are too many libraries in this area. We're selling it to make flats." He stabbed a sausage with his fork. "Very nice flats they'll be too."

"What about the people who use the library?" asked Podge. "They matter too."

"Don't be cheeky to your father," said Mrs Harris.

"It's true," Podge insisted. "People need that library. And—" Podge lowered his voice, "—Ms Wiz is going to save it."

"Did you say Wiz? Is that Wiz woman getting involved?" Mr Harris looked worried. He remembered last

term at St Barnabas when an owl
taught maths, a school inspector
found a rat in his trousers and two of
the teachers were turned into geese.
"That woman spells trouble."

"*Someone*'s got to save our books
for us," said Podge.

Mr Harris dipped his sausage into
some tomato sauce.

"Remember this, son," he said
solemnly. "Books are books – and
business is business. And never the
twain shall meet. Am I right, Mum?"

"You certainly are, Dad," said Mrs
Harris.

# CHAPTER TWO

# "Is this a library or a zoo?"

That Friday afternoon, Jack and Podge met in the park and set off for Latimer Road Library. Jack brought his skateboard, because he took his skateboard everywhere, and Podge brought a large box of sandwiches, just in case saving the library carried on over tea-time.

But when they arrived at Latimer Road, they received a shock. The library was closed and Mr Goff was sitting on the steps outside, looking miserable.

"They've locked it up," he said. "My own library and I can't get in."

"That's strange," said Jack. "It wasn't meant to be closed until tonight."

"Maybe the Chief Leisure Officer heard that your Ms Wiz had magic on her mind," said Mr Goff.

"But how?" Jack was puzzled. "It was meant to be a secret. No one would be stupid enough to blab to someone on the council, would they?"

"Well . . ." Podge was looking as if he wished he were somewhere else.

"Oh no," said Jack. "You didn't mention it to your father, did you?"

"You see—"

"Podge," said Jack wearily. "You are a complete and utter nerdbrain."

"Perhaps Ms Wiz will know what to do," said Podge weakly.

Mr Goff sniffed. "If she turns up."

"She'll be here soon," said Jack. "She'll probably fly in on her vacuum cleaner."

14

"Or just appear out of thin air," said Podge.

At that moment, the number 22 bus drew up in front of the library. Ms Wiz stepped out, carrying a plastic bag.

"Huh," said Mr Goff. "Some witch."

Ms Wiz was against giving up and going home (Mr Goff's suggestion), or smashing the door down (Jack's suggestion), or discussing the whole thing over a few sandwiches and cakes (Podge's suggestion).

"The people from the council will be here soon," she said. "After all, no one has told Mr Goff what's going to happen to him."

"What do we do when they get here?" asked Mr Goff.

"We magic 'em," said Podge with a grin.

15

"Yeah," said Jack. "Ms Wiz will use Hecate, the china cat with flashing eyes, Archie the owl and Herbert the magic rat."

"Oh, whoops!" Ms Wiz clapped a hand to her forehead. "I left them all at home."

Mr Goff, Jack and Podge looked at her in amazement.

"All right," she said with a shrug. "Nobody's perfect."

"Well, what *have* you got?" asked
Jack, beginning to wonder whether
Ms Wiz was a bit less magic than she
used to be.

Ms Wiz looked inside her plastic
bag and eventually brought out
a small bottle the size of a
pepperpot.

"I've got some Fish Powder," she
said.

"Great," said Podge. "We can

sprinkle it on my sandwiches. Fish and peanut butter. Yummy."

"And how," asked Mr Goff, "is fish powder going to save a library?"

"This is special Fish Powder," said Ms Wiz. "All we need are some books." She walked briskly towards the library door. "Ah," she said, suddenly remembering that it was locked.

"It's not your day, is it?" said Mr Goff.

Ms Wiz ignored him. "Jack," she said, "have you got any books on you?"

"Nothing much," muttered Jack. "Just a few Beatrix Potter."

"Beatrix Potter?" Podge started to laugh. "Beatrix *Potter*?"

Jack blushed. "They were for my sister," he said.

"Oh no," said Mr Goff, as a car

drew up. "Here comes Mrs Prescott, the Chief Leisure Officer."

"Quick!" shouted Ms Wiz. "Give me those books."

Jack pulled a number of small books from his jacket pocket. Ms Wiz laid them on the ground, as the Chief Leisure Officer approached.

"If you close this library down," Ms Wiz called out, reaching for her bottle of Fish Powder, "I shall not be answerable for the consequences."

"This is no longer a library," said Mrs Prescott. "It's merely a room with books in it. We shall soon remove the books so that it can be converted into flats."

"I warned you," said Ms Wiz, opening the Beatrix Potter books and sprinkling Fish Powder on their pages. There was a slight humming sound, which could be heard above the noise of the traffic on Latimer Road. Then, one by one, a succession of small animals, wearing waistcoats and pinafores, came to life and hopped out of the pages of the books and on to the pavement.

Soon Pigling Bland, the Fierce Bad Rabbit, Jemima Puddle-Duck, Peter Rabbit and several Flopsy Bunnies were hopping, waddling and scurrying about in front of the library.

"Wicked, Ms Wiz," said Jack.

"What's going on?" said Mrs Prescott. "Is this a library or a zoo?"

"This Fish Powder," said Ms Wiz, "can bring any character in a book to life." Jemima Puddle-Duck was wandering off, causing quite a stir outside the newsagent. "We can bring total confusion to this area unless you leave us our library."

"Fish Powder?" said Mrs Prescott,

stepping carefully over the Fierce Bad Rabbit.

"Right," said Ms Wiz. "FISH stands for Freeing Illustrated Storybook Heroes. It's a magic potion."

Podge and Jack gave a cheer.

Ms Wiz held up her hand. "If you don't leave this library alone, I'll release more characters. I can bring this road to a standstill."

"You won't get away with this," said Mrs Prescott, backing towards her car and nearly falling over a Flopsy Bunny in the process. "We'll be back."

She drove off quickly.

"Now," said Ms Wiz. "Let's get these animals under control."

Just then, there was a squeal of brakes from the road behind them.

"Oh no," said Podge. "That's the number 66 bus. I don't think the driver saw one of our animals."

"It's Peter Rabbit!" gasped Jack.

"Peter Rabbit? Under a bus?" Mr Goff had gone pale. "But this could change the whole shape of children's literature."

"It's certainly changed the shape of Peter Rabbit," said Podge, looking into the road.

"He was my favourite," wailed Jack.

"Don't worry," said Ms Wiz. "The Fish Powder will sort him out." She took a deep breath, sprinkled some powder on the pages of *The Tale of Peter Rabbit* and shouted, "HSIF REDWOP!"

The shape in the middle of the road disappeared. Jack looked inside his book.

"Phew!" he said. "Peter's back."

"I thought those books were for your sister," said Podge.

"Never mind that," said Ms Wiz. "We're not going to be able to change the council's mind with a few Flopsy Bunnies. What other books have you got?"

Podge reached inside his lunchbox. "How about this?" he said.

# CHAPTER THREE

# "Where exactly did you meet him, Peter?"

Mr and Mrs Harris were watching television. This was one of their favourite ways of passing the time, and Mr Harris even used to sneak home on Friday afternoons to watch *The Avenue*, the soap opera he liked most of all.

"That Maylene's heading for trouble," he said to Mrs Harris, as he sipped his tea, waiting for *The Avenue* to begin. "She shouldn't be going out with that dentist when she's already engaged to the schoolteacher."

"No," said Mrs Harris. "Not after what happened at the barbecue."

"Where's the boy?"

For a moment, Mrs Harris thought

her husband was still talking about
the dentist. Then she realized he
meant Peter, their son.

"Down at the library," she said.
"Nose in a book as usual."

"Books!" said Podge's father. "Who
needs books? When I was his age,
I didn't go filling my head with
things from books. It never did
me any harm. Turn the telly up,
Mum."

Mrs Harris turned up the volume on the television.

"Anyway," shouted Mr Harris. "We closed that library today."

"And now—" said the television announcer, '—it's time to visit *The Avenue*."

The front doorbell rang.

"That'll be Peter," said Mr Harris. He got up, grumbling. "If the bell goes at an awkward time when everyone's busy—" he opened the front door, "—it's always . . . er, good afternoon."

There, on the doorstep, was the fattest man Mr Harris had ever seen. He was wearing Bermuda shorts and a baseball cap.

"Can I help you?" asked Mr Harris nervously.

The man pointed to his mouth.

"Hi, Dad," said Podge, jumping out

from behind the giant. "This is my friend Phillip Yadzik of Chicago, USA."

Mr Harris smiled. "Howdeedodee, Phillip," he said.

"He's rather hungry," said Podge. "He's been in *The Guinness Book of Records* for the last few years."

"Well, he would be," said Mr Harris, looking puzzled.

Yadzik squeezed his way through the front door. Once inside the house, he sniffed the air like a dog at dinner-time.

"Would you like to watch *The Avenue*?" asked Mr Harris weakly. "It's just started."

"I think," said Podge, "he'd rather have a bite to eat."

Yadzik pushed his way past Mr Harris and made for the kitchen. He opened the fridge and gulped down

three chicken pies, two dozen
sausages and a family box of chips,
complete with plastic wrapping.

"Is that Peter with one of his
friends?" Mrs Harris called out from
next door.

"That's right, Mum," said Podge.

Yadzik was just swallowing a large
white loaf of bread, when Podge's
mother came out to meet him.

"Oh!" she said. Trying to look
normal when a giant is eating his way
through your kitchen isn't easy, but
somehow Mrs Harris remembered
her manners. "What a big boy you
are," she said. "Do you go to Peter's
school?"

"He doesn't talk," said Podge.
"Apparently characters freed from
books can't talk. The words belong to
their authors."

"I see," said Mrs Harris, who didn't

30

see at all. "Where exactly did you meet him, Peter?"

"In the Food and Gluttony section of *The Guinness Book of Records*. Back in 1955, he ate 77 large hamburgers in two hours. In 1957, he got through 101 bananas in fifteen minutes. But he hasn't eaten for several years, so those records are probably about to be broken."

"Our Sunday lunch," squealed Mrs Harris, as Yadzik found a chicken in the freezer and, with a great crunching noise, sank his teeth into it.

"I don't think he can wait until Sunday," said Podge.

"He's going to eat us out of house and home," said Mr Harris. "Tell him to go away, Peter – please."

"Oh dear," said Podge. "He's going into the front room. I wonder what he'll eat there."

Yadzik sat down heavily on the sofa, breaking all its legs. He casually reached for a cushion and started eating at it.

"He may eat you out of house and home," said Podge casually. "But he'll probably eat the house and home first."

"What are we going to do?" said Mr Harris. Podge had never seen his father look so helpless before.

"The thing is," he answered, as Yadzik tore down a curtain and began chewing one end. "Phillip used to be just a picture in a book. That was his home."

"Yeees?" said Mr Harris, looking puzzled.

"And now someone is closing down the library, where his book was kept. It's the Latimer Road Library."

"Go on," said Mr Harris suspiciously.

"So if someone could just *open* the library," Podge continued, "I'm sure Phillip would be happy to go home. In fact, Ms Wiz just has to sprinkle some powder on his pages and say some funny words and he'll be back in the book, just another weird record."

"Ms Wiz!" said Mr Harris. "I might have known that she'd be involved."

There was a cracking noise as Yadzik crushed a table and started picking at the legs like a smaller person might eat chips.

"I'll ring Mrs Prescott," said Mr Harris, picking up the phone and dialling. "Try and distract him with the television, Mum."

"I wouldn't do that," said Podge.

"Hullo," said Mr Harris into the

telephone. "Is that Mrs Prescott, the Chief Leisure Officer? This is Councillor Cuthbert Harris. I want you to open the Latimer Road Library. Yes, this afternoon. It's an emergency."

"Now, Phillip," Mrs Harris was saying. "How about a bit of television?"

"I really don't think that's a good idea," said Podge.

The giant looked at Mrs Harris for a moment. Then his eyes shifted to the television and he smiled.

"No, I'm not drunk," Mr Harris was shouting into the phone. "This Ms Wiz is releasing characters from books. They're everywhere! Hullo? Mrs Prescott? Are you there?"

Yadzik walked over to the television, took out the plug and

picked it up with a hungry grunt. He licked his lips.

"Not the television!" screamed Mr Harris, dropping the phone. "You can eat anything but that! NOOOOOOOO!"

CHAPTER FOUR

# "PWOBLEM?"

"Um . . ."

Mr Goff had never been a very brave man. In fact, he was extremely nervous. That was why he had become a librarian. Books were easier to deal with than people. They didn't answer back, or make a noise, or call you names behind your back.

"Um, excuse me . . ."

That is, until Ms Wiz came along with her Fish Powder. It was all very well saving the library by Freeing Illustrated Storybook Characters, but once people from books started walking about the place, living their own lives, where would it all end?

"Um, excuse me, I say . . ."

In trouble. That's where it would
end. Mr Goff tried to imagine what
Latimer Road Library would be like,
if this Fish Powder was being
scattered about. Ms Wiz had said
that they couldn't talk when they
were outside the pages of their
books, but what would happen if
someone brought *The History of
the Second World War* to life? Or
*Great Whales of the World*? Or – a

terrible thought occurred to him
– the rude pictures in some of the
Sunday papers? It would cause a
riot.

"Um, excuse me, I say, would you
mind listening . . .?"

Ms Wiz, Jack and Podge continued
to ignore Mr Goff as, standing
outside the library, they discussed
what to do next.

"SSSSHHHH!"

At last, they all turned round and
noticed that the librarian was trying
to say something.

"It seems to me," said Mr Goff,
"that this is all getting a bit out of
control."

"Not really," said Podge. "Peter
Rabbit's back in his book. Ms Wiz
returned Phillip to Food and Gluttony
by sprinkling Fish Powder on his
lines and saying 'HSIF REDWOP'

before he ate my house. Shame about the television, though."

"Don't you want to save your library?" asked Jack.

"Of course, I do," said Mr Goff. "But are squashed rabbits and hamburger-crazed Americans really going to help us? Mrs Prescott will simply call the police and that will be that."

"I suppose you're right," said Ms Wiz.

"We need to change Mrs Prescott's mind somehow," said Mr Goff.

"I don't know how," said Ms Wiz. "The library's closed and we haven't got any more books to bring to life."

"Unless—" Mr Goff looked more embarrassed than ever as he reached into his briefcase "—you can use this."

He gave a picture book to Ms Wiz.

"Well done, Mr Goff," she said smiling.

"I was always a bit of a fan of their majesties," he said.

Podge looked at the book.

"I don't get it," he said. "How on earth can *The Bumper Book of Royal Weddings* help us?"

When Caroline Smith received a telephone call from her friend Jack, asking for her help, she wasn't a bit surprised.

"Not homework again?" she said.

"We need someone who can do voices," said Jack. "You're the best actress I know. See you at the Town Hall in ten minutes."

"Hang on," said Caroline. "Who's we?"

"Me, Podge – and Ms Wiz."

Caroline gave a little whoop of delight. "I'll be there," she said.

It had been a very normal day for Mrs Prescott, the Chief Leisure Officer. The only interesting thing to happen was a rather odd call from Cuthbert Harris – something about the Latimer Road Library and his television being eaten – which she had ignored. Cuthbert sometimes enjoyed a drink or three at lunchtime. It was probably his idea of a joke.

There was a knock at the door.

"Come in," said Mrs Prescott.

"I . . . but . . . if . . . sir . . . help . . ." It was her secretary Mrs Simpson, who seemed to be having trouble speaking.

"What on *earth* is the matter, Mrs Simpson?"

"Wheah is the Chief Lejaah Orficer?" said a loud voice from next door. "I *demaaaand* to see her!"

The door burst open to reveal the most unusual visitors Mrs Prescott had ever received.

"It's their Royal Highnesses," said Mrs Simpson, recovering her voice at last. "A famous prince and princess from Buckingham Palace. They're making a surprise visit to the Town Hall."

"We're gaying walkabout, aaahn't

we, deah?" said the voice coming
from the princess.

"Don't overdo the accent," Jack
whispered to Caroline as they stood,
with Podge, Ms Wiz and Mr Goff,
behind the royal couple. It was lucky,
he thought, that the princess was in
her wedding dress and wore a veil
over her face. No one could see that
her mouth wasn't moving with
Caroline's words.

"Are you the Chief Lejaah
Orficer?"

"Yes, ma'am." Mrs Prescott was
hurriedly tidying the papers on her
desk, while trying to curtsey at the
same time. "At your service, ma'am."

The prince, smiling his royal smile,
shook her hand.

"Tell meah, may good womaaan,"
continued Caroline in her princess
voice. "How is may favouwite libway,

45

the Latimaaah Woad Libway? Ay *love* weading."

Mrs Prescott winced. "It's c-c-c-closed," she said eventually.

"AY BIG YOUR PAAAHDON?"

"We . . . I've just closed it down, ma'am."

"May favouwite libway? I wed may vair farst book theah."

Mrs Prescott looked confused.

"I think," said Jack helpfully, "that Her Royal Highness is saying that she read her very first book there."

"Yah," said Caroline.

"Did you, ma'am?" Mrs Prescott was unable to hide her surprise. Somehow the princess didn't look as if she came from the Latimer Road area.

"Ay *demaaaand* that you aypen it. This vair afternoon."

Mrs Prescott gulped.

46

"We can't aypen – I mean open it,"
she said. "We've only just closed it. It
would be a problem."

"PWOBLEM?" Caroline's voice hit
a new high note. "Well, if you can't
aypen it, we jolly well shall. Shaaan't
we, Pwincey?"

The prince was still smiling his
royal smile and shaking hands with
everyone. He now stood where

Caroline was crouched behind the princess. He smiled and held out his hand.

"Leave off, prince," muttered Podge. "I think she's a bit busy at present."

"Ay'm gaying theah wight now," said Caroline. "Ay maight even mention you in may speech when ay aypen the libway."

"Speech?" said Jack under his breath. "I don't believe it."

"Thank you, ma'am." Mrs Prescott gave a little bob of the head.

"So the Latimah Woad Libway will be aypen again, awight? And stay aypen, OK?"

"Yes, Your Royal Highness," said Mrs Prescott.

"Yeah!" said Jack, rather too loudly.

Mrs Prescott looked up sharply.

48

"Sorry, ma'am, did you say something?"

"Yah," said Caroline quickly. "OK, yah."

"Ma'am," said Mrs Prescott, blushing. "May I ask Your Royal Highness why you appear to be wearing your wedding dress."

There was a moment's pause.

"Because ... Ectually ..." Caroline was thinking fast. "Because it's may anniverseway. So theah!"

And with that, the royal couple, followed by Caroline, Jack, Podge, Mr Goff and Ms Wiz, swept out of the room.

# CHAPTER FIVE

# "Frankenstein comes to Latimer Road"

It took quite a long time for the royal party to walk from the Town Hall to Latimer Road because the prince insisted on shaking hands with everyone they met.

"May wedding dwess is getting dusty," said Caroline at one point. "Could you be bwidesmaid and pick it up for me, Podge?"

"You must be joking," said Podge. "Anyway what are you going to say in your speech?"

Caroline laughed. "Ay'll think of something," she said.

A few steps behind them, Mr Goff was walking with Ms Wiz.

"I can't help noticing," he said,

"that you don't seem to be your normal happy self."

Ms Wiz sighed. "You were right, Mr Goff," she said. "It's not my day."

"But why not? The library's going to be re-opened."

"If I tell you something, will you promise not to panic?"

Mr Goff nodded.

"I've lost the Fish Powder. I think someone's taken it."

"Oh dear." Mr Goff started panicking. For some reason, he started thinking about the Second World War. Great Whales of the World. The rude pictures in the Sunday papers. "Oh *dear*!" he said.

By the time the royal couple had reached Latimer Road, there was quite a crowd following them. Waiting for them at the library was Mrs Prescott, who had driven there as

quickly as possible and hung a pink
ribbon across the doorway.

"Your Highnesses *walked*?" she said
with disbelief in her voice.

Caroline crouched down behind
the princess once more.

"We laik to meet the common
people," she said loudly.

"Common?" said Jack. "That's
nice."

Mrs Prescott gave the princess a
pair of scissors.

"If you would be so kind as to cut
the ribbon, Your Highness," she said,
"we can then open the library."

The princess took the scissors.
Behind her, Caroline shouted,
"Thenks to the efforts of your
soopah Chief Lejaah Orficer Mrs
Prescott, and to your divaine
libwawian Mr Goff, not to mention
the absolutely spiffing Ms Wiz,

ay can declare this libway well and twuly aypen!"

Everyone cheered as the princess cut the ribbon and, closely followed by her prince and Caroline, walked into the library.

Soon the place was as busy as ever. The princess sat down with a group of five-year-olds who were being read a story. The prince shook hands with the old man who was settling back into his favourite armchair.

"Ms Wiz," said Podge. "I think it's Fish Powder time. If you don't return the prince and princess to their book soon, Mrs Prescott's going to get suspicious. Caroline can't keep that voice up much longer."

"Now where *is* that Fish Powder?" said Ms Wiz, rummaging in her plastic bag. "It could really be most embarrassing if it fell into the wrong hands."

Just then a woman fainted at the far end of the library. Standing next to her, looking slightly confused, was a ghost.

"Where has Jack got to?" Ms Wiz asked suddenly.

Podge shrugged. "I think I saw him in the Horror and Ghost section," he said.

"And where's that?"

"Behind where that monster with three heads has just appeared out of thin air."

"*Oh no!*" said Ms Wiz.

Soon the library was in total confusion, with spirits, zombies, werewolves and vampires wandering in and out of the shelves. There were screams of alarm as men, women and children stampeded towards the door. Even the prince and princess looked rather surprised.

"Wow," said Podge. "Frankenstein comes to Latimer Road."

"It's all right," Ms Wiz was shouting. "They can't harm you. They're not real, I promise!"

But no one listened to her.

"Sorreee," said Jack, ambling up to her with the bottle of Fish Powder in his hand. "I just wanted to see if it worked."

Without a word, Ms Wiz took the

bottle and sprinkled powder over the pages Jack had opened.

"HSIF REDWOP!" she shouted. "HSIF REDWOP!"

Gradually, the library was cleared as the demons returned to the books from which they had come.

"I've seen everything now," said Mrs Prescott, who had turned quite white. "A royal visit, then Frankenstein in Latimer

Road. I'm glad I don't work here."

"So you won't close us again?" asked Mr Goff.

"Certainly not," said Mrs Prescott, backing out of the door. "This is your library, Mr Goff – and you're welcome to it. Goodbye."

Mr Goff turned to Ms Wiz. "Could I have my *Bumper Book of Royal Weddings* back now?" he asked.

"Of course," said Ms Wiz. "Let me just put the royal couple back." She sprinkled some Fish Powder on to the book and said, "HSIF REDWOP."

The prince and princess started to fade. The last Jack, Podge and Caroline saw of them was a royal smile.

"What a charming couple," said Ms Wiz, giving Mr Goff back his book. "Now, I'd better be off myself."

"Can't you stay?" said Mr Goff.

"The library won't be the same without you."

"Of course it will," said Ms Wiz. "You're the best librarian I've ever met."

Mr Goff blushed.

"Anyway," said Caroline. "Ms Wiz always comes back. She goes wherever magic's needed."

"That's right, Caroline," said Ms Wiz. "Cheerio, everyone."

She held the bottle of Fish Powder high in the air and tapped some out on to her head. "HSIF REDWOP," she said. She smiled, gave a little wave – and faded away.

For the first time in Mr Goff's memory, there was complete silence in the library.

"Whaaaaat?" said Podge eventually. "That means that Ms Wiz is a character in a story."

There was another silence.

"And if she comes from a book," said Caroline, "then where does that leave us?"

"Don't even *think* about it," said Jack.

# MS WIZ
# GOES LIVE

# CHAPTER ONE
# Parent Problems

It was an evening like any other at the Smith household.

Mr Smith was in the living room reading a newspaper and drinking a can of beer. Mrs Smith was shouting at him from the kitchen. Caroline, their eldest child, was trying to do her homework and wondering what it was about parents that made them argue all the time. And her three-year-old sister, known to everyone as Little Musha, was in front of the television, carefully working some chocolate cake into the carpet.

There was a crash of cutlery from the kitchen.

"I work all day!" Mrs Smith said loudly. "And have you done the

washing-up when I come home, or cooked the children's supper, or done the hoovering or made the beds? Have you heck!"

"Yak yak yak," said Mr Smith, taking a swig of beer. "I've been out looking for a job. I'm tired."

Caroline sighed and took the remains of the chocolate cake from her little sister, who started crying.

There was another crash of plates from the kitchen. "All I can say," muttered Mrs Smith, "is that you've changed. You're not the man I married."

"That's true," said Mr Smith. "I was happy then."

"Happy!" Mrs Smith gave an angry laugh. "You've always been a miserable useless, lazy—"

"Mum," said Caroline, who knew exactly when to interrupt her parents' rows. "I'm trying to do my homework and Musha keeps trying to turn the television on."

"It's my favourite programme," said Musha.

"What is?" asked Caroline.

Musha thought for a moment. "Whatever's on now," she said.

"*Please* tell her, Mum—"

"STOP FIGHTING!" Their mother stamped her foot. A plate fell to the ground and smashed. There was silence for a moment. Mrs Smith sighed. "Let her watch television, Caro," she said. "At least, we get some peace that way."

"What about my homework?"

Mr Smith wandered into the kitchen. "I'm going to the pub," he mumbled.

"The *pub*?" gasped Mrs Smith.

"Why don't you both go out?" said Caroline, quickly joining them.

"Great idea," said her mother

tearfully. "We could go and watch a terrible film and grumble about it afterwards or eat at a restaurant and realize we have nothing to say to one another, or just watch other people having fun in a pub."

Mr Smith put his arm around his wife's shoulders. "Come on, love," he said. "Let's have an evening out. We both need a break."

"And what about a babysitter?" asked Mrs Smith.

Just then the doorbell rang. Caroline opened the door.

"Good evening," said a young woman with a clipboard under her arm. "I'm doing a survey for—"

"Ms Wiz!" Caroline smiled. "What on earth are you doing here?"

"I'm doing a survey for—"

"Hey, Mum, Dad," Caroline shouted over her shoulder. "This is Ms Wiz, who did all the magic things

at school and visited Jack in hospital and found Lizzie's stolen cat and saved the library by bringing Peter Rabbit and Frankenstein to life."

"Not that witch woman?" said Mr Smith suspiciously.

"Paranormal Operative actually," said Ms Wiz. "It's not quite the same."

"Can Paranormal Operatives babysit?" asked Mrs Smith.

"Well," said Ms Wiz. "I'm really here to complete this survey."

"What's it about, Ms Wiz?" asked Caroline. "Something magic?"

Ms Wiz looked at the clipboard and took a deep breath. "I need to know how many windows people have in their houses, how big the windows are, if they're happy with their windows and, if not, how they would like them changed, whether their windows go up and down or open sideways or slide, if they're draughty when the wind blows, whether they're made of wood or metal, how often the window cleaner comes, how much he charges, how many windows *he* has at home, does he wash them with a sponge or a cloth or bits of newspaper and does he whistle while he works and—"

"Boring," said Little Musha.

"I suppose it is rather," said Ms Wiz. "All right. I'll babysit for you." She stepped into the house.

"Are you reliable?" asked Mrs Smith.

"Reliable?" Caroline laughed. "She was a teacher. You can't be more reliable than that, can you?"

"Mmm," said Mr Smith uncertainly. "Wasn't there something about her keeping a rat up her sleeve?"

"That was just a rumour," said Caroline, handing her father his coat

and holding the front door open for him. "You both go out and enjoy yourselves."

Mumbling, Mr and Mrs Smith made their way out of the house. As Ms Wiz, Caroline and Little Musha waved them goodbye, they were arguing as to how they should spend the evening.

"Phew!" said Ms Wiz, closing the front door. She pulled a rat out of her sleeve. "Can Herbert have a run now?"

"Survey, eh?" said Caroline with a smile. "You knew I needed help."

Ms Wiz shrugged. "I go where magic's needed," she said. "So what's the problem here?"

Caroline frowned. "I always seem to be sorting things out. Musha, Mummy, Daddy. I'm only nine but I never have any fun these days."

"We'll see about that," said Ms Wiz.

Herbert, the magic rat, was scurrying towards the kitchen when Little Musha picked him up rather roughly.

"Don't like rats," she said, nose to nose with Herbert.

Ms Wiz smiled. "Not even rats with miniature water-pistols in their right ears?"

"What?" said Little Musha.

At that moment a jet of water

squirted from Herbert's right ear, hitting Little Musha in the eye. "Ow!" she shouted, dropping the rat and starting to cry.

When Little Musha cried, the glasses in the kitchen rattled, the neighbours shut their windows and cats disappeared up trees in terror at the noise. It was like a police siren.

"This is Little Musha," Caroline

shouted to Ms Wiz. "She's—"
Caroline remembered a phrase that
grown-ups liked to use when
discussing her sister "—she's quite a
character."

"Little Musha, eh?" said Ms Wiz.
"Is that a nice Indian name?"

Little Musha stopped crying. "I'm
called Musha," she said, treading on
Ms Wiz's toe, "because I mush
people."

"Her real name's Annie," Caroline
explained. "But she's going through
a mushing phase and likes to be called
Little Musha."

"Well, she had better not mush
me," said Ms Wiz firmly. "And what
are we going to do tonight, Little
Musha?"

"Television."

"Oh no," said Caroline. "We could
do amazing things now that Ms Wiz
is here. She can turn people into

animals, make things disappear. She can fly."

Musha thought for a moment. "Television," she said.

"See?" said Caroline. "No fun."

"What's wrong with television?" asked Ms Wiz.

"But we always watch—"

Ms Wiz held up her hand and smiled. "Trust me," she said.

CHAPTER TWO

# Jimmy goes Bananas

"You're getting *smaller*, Ms Wiz!"

Caroline and Ms Wiz were watching the What-a-Load-of-Show-Offs Show on television when Little Musha began to stare at Ms Wiz.

"It's true," she said. "You really are getting smaller, Ms Wiz."

"Yes," said Ms Wiz. "I'm thinking of going into television."

"Oh no," said Caroline, who now saw that her sister was right and that Ms Wiz was shrinking rapidly. "Don't go all small on us. You're meant to be babysitting."

Ms Wiz was now slightly smaller than Little Musha. "You can shrink too, if you like," she said.

"But then what happens?" asked Caroline.

"We enjoy some television, from inside the television set."

"Yeah!" said Little Musha. "Do it, Ms Wiz."

When Ms Wiz was around, the strangest things seemed normal. Within seconds, Caroline discovered that the furniture in her living room appeared to have grown to an enormous size. A fly on a wall nearby looked as big as a jumbo jet.

"Follow me," said Ms Wiz to Caroline and Little Musha. They all climbed on to a nearby matchstick.

"Hold tight," shouted Ms Wiz as the sound of a low hum filled the room. The matchstick hovered above the ground and then carried the three of them on to the television set.

"What about Herbert?" asked Caroline.

"It's all right," said Ms Wiz.
"He's in my pocket – as tiny as
we are."

"I hate Herbert," muttered Little
Musha, remembering the water
pistol. "I hope he disappears
altogether."

"Now how exactly are we going to
get into this set?" Ms Wiz was
tapping the top of the television.
"Here we are," she said, opening a

small trapdoor. Some steps led into the dark inside.

Little Musha gasped. "Ms Wiz is going into the telly," she said. "What are we going to do now?"

Caroline remembered that she was meant to be the responsible one. "But we're not even allowed to touch the back of the television because it's so dangerous," she shouted down the steps. "I don't think Mum and Dad would like it if we got right inside."

"Don't worry," Ms Wiz's voice echoed in the darkness. "This is magic TV."

"Come on then," said Little Musha.

Caroline sighed, took her little sister's hand and stepped into the television set.

"Ready?" said Ms Wiz, when they reached the bottom of the steps. In front of them was a large door with a notice saying "STUDIO 5 – DO NOT

ENTER WHEN THE RED LIGHT IS ON". The red light above the door shone brightly.

"What's the light for?" asked Caroline.

"It means they're making a programme," said Ms Wiz. "It's probably the one we were watching. Let's go in and see."

She opened the door and all three of them were dazzled by bright lights.

"And now," a voice was saying, "the What-a-Load-of-Show-Offs Show welcomes our next contestant."

As her eyes grew accustomed to the studio lights, Caroline saw a man with a yellow jersey walking towards them.

"It's Jimmy," she whispered. "He's the star of What-a-Load-of-Show-Offs."

"Yes," said Ms Wiz. "And we're on his show."

"I want to go home," said Little
Musha.

Jimmy took her hand and held it
tightly. "Hello, little girl," he said,
putting his face close to Little
Musha's. "And what's our name
then?"

"Musha."

"Musha." Jimmy winked at the
camera which had followed him
across the studio. "What a lovely

name. Why do they call you that?"

"Careful," Caroline murmured, but it was too late.

"Because I like mushing." Little Musha reached out for Jimmy's nose and twisted it hard.

"Aaaaagghh!" The star of What-a-Load-of-Show-Offs hopped from one foot to the other until Little Musha let go of his nose. "Aaaaggghhh...
ha...ha...ha...Isn't live television great, folks?"

"Why have you got tears in your eyes?" asked Little Musha.

"I'll tell you after the show," said Jimmy through clenched teeth.
"Come over here and play our lovely quiz game."

Ms Wiz and Caroline took a seat at the back of the studio as Little Musha reluctantly allowed herself to be led to a big chair.

"Now every time I say a word,"

said Jimmy. "You have to say another word that's a bit like it. So I say 'rain' and you say 'cloud' or 'sun' or 'wet'. All right?"

Little Musha nodded. Her chin was set like a boxer's before a fight. This was never a good sign.

Jimmy smiled. "Now—"

"Then," said Little Musha.

"I haven't started yet, *silly*."

"Billy," said Little Musha.

"No—"

"Yes."

"Very funny," said Jimmy, whose face was now a bright red colour. "The first word is . . . hair."

"Pull."

"Ice cream."

"Carpet."

"Bedtime."

"Scream."

"Toe."

"Stamp."

"Stamp?" said Jimmy. "That's
not right, is it? Now where's the
connection between toe and—"

Little Musha brought her sharp
little heel down hard on Jimmy's toe.

"EEEERRRRGGGGHHHH!"
Jimmy staggered back. "Where's a
doctor? Where's my agent? Get this
child out of here! I never wanted to
work with children anyway. I was
going to be an actor."

"I think we've outstayed our welcome," said Ms Wiz quietly to Caroline. "Get your sister and follow me."

"Someone take this little brute away," Jimmy was shouting.

Caroline hurried forward and grabbed Musha.

"That was fun," said Little Musha.

"Maybe for you," said Caroline, dragging her out of the studio. "For me, it's home from home. Now come *on*."

Ms Wiz was waiting for them at a door marked "EXIT".

"Don't like Jimmy," said Little Musha as they hurried out of the studio.

Ms Wiz sighed. "I don't think he's wild about you either," she said.

# CHAPTER THREE

# "No autographs, perlease!"

"No, of course you're not a little brute," said Caroline, holding Musha's hand as they hurried along a brightly-lit corridor. "Is she, Ms Wiz?"

"Certainly not," said Ms Wiz.

"Where are we going to now?" asked Little Musha.

"Let's try and find a programme with a bit less violence," said Ms Wiz. "If we go on like this, we could get banned from the television."

Caroline had an idea. "Maybe I could—"

"Hey," shouted Little Musha as they turned a corner. "Cartoons!"

"Oh, forget it," sighed Caroline.

Ahead of them, standing outside a

studio door, sipping tea, were two cartoon characters, a cat and a mouse.

Little Musha gasped. "It's Tom and Jerry," she said.

Jerry, the cartoon mouse, gave a weary smile. "No autographs, perlease," he said. "Not when we're resting between takes."

"I thought that Tom and you were meant to be enemies," said Caroline. "On television, you're always chasing each other about and hitting one another over the head."

"Don't believe everything you see on the screen," said Jerry. "We're enemies when the cameras roll but in real life, we're buddies."

"Real life!" Caroline smiled. "But you're cartoon characters."

"Hey, lady," said Jerry, putting on his well-known frown. "Don't knock cartoons, perlease. Like this evening, we're rehearsing a scene where Tom's

playing golf. He rolls me up into a
little ball and wallops me three
hundred yards. I bounce off a tree,
rebound off a passing seagull, catch
Tom in the stomach and flatten him
against a wall, which then collapses
on top of him."

"You *rehearse* that?" asked Caroline.

"How else d'you think we get it
right?" said Tom. "Magic?"

"The producer says we could use
stand-ins but we like to do our own
stunts," said Jerry. "Talking of which,
it's time for me to run Tom over with
a steamroller."

Tom winked. "Showbiz!" he said.
"Don't you just love it?"

"Can I come?" asked Little Musha.

"No," said Ms Wiz and Caroline
at the same time. Musha took a
deep breath, sniffed a couple of
times and burst into tears at
maximum volume.

A woman hurried down the corridor towards them.

"*Ssshhh!*" she went. "How can we make television programmes with that terrible din? We've already had a disaster tonight with Jimmy throwing a tantrum on the What-a-Load-of-Show-Offs Show."

"Oh dear," said Ms Wiz, trying to keep a straight face. "We wouldn't know about that. We're just here on a visit."

"And what exactly are you here to see?" asked the woman.

Caroline put up a hand. "I was hoping—"

"We're looking for a really nice show," Ms Wiz interrupted.

"Nice?" The woman scratched her head. "There's not much demand for that these days. I suppose you could try our new series, Wild, Woolly and Weally Intewesting. They're doing a programme on extinct species at the moment, downstairs in Studio 9B."

The red light outside Studio 9B was shining brightly and there was a sign on the door which said, "QUIET! EXTINCT ANIMALS – DO NOT DISTURB!"

"What does extinct mean?" asked Little Musha.

"It means that they're the type of animals that no longer exist in the world," said Caroline.

"How can they be disturbed then?"

"I think it's a sort of television joke," said Ms Wiz, gently pushing the studio door open.

"Wow!" said Caroline.

Studio 9B had been decorated like a jungle, full of trees and creepers and the sound of exotic birds. In the centre of the studio, a big man with a beard was talking breathlessly in front of a camera.

"And so," he said. "Over litewally hundweds of centuwies, species changed, evolved and adapted to the world's enviwonment. If they haven't changed, many of them have pewished, died out, become extinct. Like—" the man walked across the studio to where a model of a strange-looking animal stood "—like Tywannosauwus Wex."

"Why aren't the animals moving?" whispered Little Musha.

"Because they're extinct," said Caroline.

A faint humming noise was coming from Ms Wiz. "I wonder if this programme needs livening up," she said.

"And then," the bearded man continued, "there's the dodo, a bird that died out almost two hundwed years ago." He walked to where Ms

Wiz stood. "Here we have a stuffed model of the dodo – as you can see, it's vewy vewy dead and extinct."

At that moment, the dodo put its head on one side and pecked at something on the studio floor.

"Now that's weally wather stwange," said the bearded man nervously. "Extinct animals don't usually move like that."

The dodo flapped its wings and flew on to a branch. "*Vewy* odd,' said the television presenter, scratching his beard. "The dodo can't fly. Or couldn't fly. I think I must be dweaming."

"Off you go, Herbert," muttered Ms Wiz, releasing the magic rat from her sleeve. Herbert stood on her arm, then spread his front legs and started to fly, like a small bird. After circling around Ms Wiz a couple of times, he flew across the studio.

The bearded man was climbing the tree towards the dodo when he noticed Herbert, hovering delicately a few inches away from his nose.

"Good gwacious me!" he said with a hint of panic in his voice. "This looks vewy like a type of humming-bird, except it's a wat – it's a sort of humming-wat." He sat down heavily on a branch. "I must be ill. I'm seeing things," he said. "Turn the wuddy camewas off."

"Cut!" The loud shout came from a man in shirtsleeves who was now hurrying across the studio.

"What on earth's going on?" he asked.

"The dodo was alive," said the bearded man weakly. "Then I was buzzed by a humming-wat."

"The dodo?' The man in shirtsleeves looked up at the tree, where now the stuffed dodo was standing lifelessly. "Who put it up there?"

"It flew," moaned the bearded man. "And then I saw a humming-wat."

"Come on," said Ms Wiz, quietly putting Herbert up her sleeve. "I think it's time for us all to leave the jungle."

"So why don't you magic lots of extinct animals back to life?" Caroline asked after they had crept out of Studio 9B. "I'd love to see a real live dinosaur."

"My spells don't last that long," said Ms Wiz. "A few minutes at the mo—"

"Excuse me," said a woman, hurrying down the corridor towards them. "Are you the replacement newsreader?"

"Newsreader?" said Ms Wiz. "Ah, yes. That's me."

"Andrew, our normal reader, has a terrible cold and has completely lost his voice," said the woman. "You're on the air in five minutes so you had all better follow me."

"News?" said Caroline. "I thought we were here for fun."

"We are," said Ms Wiz. "I think this could be tremendous fun."

"But what about—?"

"Right," said Ms Wiz, turning to the woman. "Where's my studio?" she said.

# CHAPTER FOUR

# Good News for Really Nice People

"It's coming up to ten o'clock and, in a few seconds' time, we'll be going over to the newsroom for the news, read by Dolores Wisdom."

Caroline and Little Musha sat in a small room next door to where Ms Wiz was about to read the news and watched her through a big window between the two rooms. Beside them sat the producer, who was looking very nervous.

"She has done this before, hasn't she?" he asked Caroline.

"Probably," said Caroline.

"Because once she's started, we can't interrupt her, you know," warned the producer. "This is going out live."

"I'm sure she'll make it really . . . entertaining," said Caroline.

"Entertaining?" The producer looked more worried than ever. "I just want her to read the words on the little screen in front of her." He looked at a clock on the wall.

"Cue, Miss Wisdom," he said, holding his hand up.

"Good evening," said Ms Wiz, wearing her most serious expression

and reading the words in front of her.
"It's ten o'clock and here are the
news headlines. There has been a
plane crash in Italy. The economy is
looking worse than ever. The
government says it's everyone else's
fault. More wind and rain are forecast
throughout the country. A famous
actor has died. And—" Ms Wiz
hesitated for a moment and said,
"This is all a bit depressing, isn't it?"

"Hang on," said the producer next door. "Depressing? That wasn't in the script."

"You can hear all the gloomy news somewhere else," said Ms Wiz with a smile. "In the meantime, here's the good news for really nice people. Mr and Mrs Smith of 91 Elmtree Road went out tonight and had a very enjoyable time—"

"Whaaaaat?" said the producer. "Has she gone mad?"

"This," continued Ms Wiz, "after a grim start to the evening, during which Mrs Smith called Mr Smith miserable and lazy and then broke a plate—"

"How did she know that?" asked Little Musha.

"Listening at the door, probably," said Caroline.

"—but all has ended well, with the Smiths enjoying some fish and chips, just like the old days, followed by a romantic walk in the park. Their children, Caroline and Musha, have been shrunk by the babysitter."

The producer was now standing in front of the window and waving wildly at Ms Wiz, who waved back before going on with the news.

"Rats are getting nicer, it was officially announced tonight. And we have a rat spokesperson with us in the studio." Ms Wiz pulled Herbert the rat out of her sleeve. "So, Mr Herbert," she said. "Why have you rats suddenly decided to clean up your act?"

"Basically," said Herbert, looking towards the camera, "we're tired of the bad publicity. People say we're unfriendly, dirty and spread diseases and frankly, at the end of the day, this is not what we're about."

"And so what will you be doing about it?"

"First of all, we'll be cleaning our teeth," said Herbert. "There's no doubt that bright yellow teeth in a rat gives a very bad first impression. Then we'll be taking baths every day, and generally coming out of the closet and joining family life, rolling playfully around on the carpet, playing with the kids and so on."

"What about cats?" asked Ms Wiz.

"That's still a bit of a grey area," said Herbert. "But we hope to negotiate a peace settlement with them very soon."

"Thank you, Mr Herbert," said Ms Wiz, opening her sleeve so that he could return home. "That's really nice news."

"I've had enough," said the producer, getting to his feet. "I'm going to shut that woman up and read the news myself."

"And there's also good news for Paranormal Operatives," Ms Wiz was saying, when the producer walked briskly into the news studio. He was just about to lift Ms Wiz out of her chair when viewers throughout the country heard a faint humming noise. There was a flash of smoke – and there, in the place of the producer, stood a panda, blinking its eyes in the studio lights.

"We've just received a late news flash," said Ms Wiz. "A television producer has been turned into a panda. As everyone knows, the panda is a threatened species. In fact—" Ms Wiz pulled the panda's ear "—I'm threatening this one right now."

The panda slunk miserably out of the studio.

"Can I have a ride?" asked Little Musha, climbing on its broad back as it returned to the control room.

"As I was saying," Ms Wiz smiled at the camera, "the good news for Paranormal Operatives is that the word 'witch' is to be banned from dictionaries. I asked a well-known Paranormal Operative – me – why the ban was necessary. 'Well,' I answered myself, 'the word "witch"

suggests to a lot of people that to be
magic you have to be an ugly old
woman with cobwebs in your hair.
This, of course, isn't true.' 'Why not?'
I asked. 'Because,' I replied, 'magic
belongs to all ages and to men as well
as women, although, between me and
me, women are rather better at it.'
'Thank you, Ms Wiz'," said Ms Wiz.

   "This is getting very strange,"
said Caroline.

"Finally news of a really nice record achieved today. Little Musha Smith of 91 Elmtree Road has stayed up after ten o'clock and only burst into tears once. 'We're really proud of her,' said sister Caroline. 'Apart from pulling Jimmy's nose and then stamping on his foot, she has been an angel'."

"Hey, Musha," Caroline called out. "You're on the news."

But Little Musha was too busy riding the panda to pay any attention.

"Typical," sighed Caroline.

# CHAPTER FIVE

# A Lovely Perf

For a girl who had spent the evening inside her parents' television set with her favourite Paranormal Operative and a little sister who was now behaving quite well, Caroline was feeling surprisingly sad.

"Heigh-ho," Ms Wiz was saying, as they wandered along yet another corridor. "I really enjoyed that."

"You did seem to be having quite a lot of fun," said Caroline pointedly. "Just like Little Musha had quite a lot of fun earlier. Almost everyone has been having fun."

Ms Wiz smiled. "Anyway," she said, "we'd better head back to the real world. Your mum and dad will be home soon."

"I'm going to tell them about pulling Jimmy's nose," said Little Musha.

"What about my newsreading?" Ms Wiz laughed. "I always wanted to do that. The producer was quite upset about it."

"He'd still be galumphing about as a panda if I hadn't reminded you to turn him back into a producer," said Caroline quietly.

"Yes, thank goodness you were there," said Ms Wiz.

"I'm always there," said Caroline grumpily. "It's just like home in this television set. I keep Musha out of trouble. I even have to sort things out when the great Ms Wiz is having a good time. Why have I always got to be sensible and grown-up? When is it my turn to enjoy myself?"

Ms Wiz gave a little smile as they

walked past a door marked "GREEN ROOM".

"That's where the actors rest," she said. "Hey, you like acting, don't you, Caroline? Would you like to see if there's anyone there?"

Caroline shrugged. "If you like," she said.

Ms Wiz opened the door to reveal a man and a woman in Victorian costume. They both were pacing backwards and forwards and seemed rather upset.

"Wow," whispered Caroline. "It's Nigel Triffroll and Dulcima de Trop, the famous actors."

"What have I *always* said?" Nigel was clasping his brow. "Never agree to act with children or animals."

"And that ghastly little Jane was a bit of both," said Dulcima, fanning herself with a copy of *The Stage*.

"Very droll, darling," said Nigel.

"What appears to be the trouble?" asked Ms Wiz.

The two actors turned to them without showing the least surprise.

"Only that the little brute of a small girl who was supposed to appear in the last episode of Heritage, our wonderful costume drama, has got tonsillitis," said Dulcima.

"Tonsillitis, hah!" cried Nigel with a dismissive wave of the arm. "Otherwise known as stage fright."

"Why don't I do it?" asked
Caroline.

Nigel and Dulcima looked at her in
amazement.

"Are you a thesp?" asked Nigel.

"A what?"

Nigel sighed with impatience. "Do
you tread the boards?" he said.

"If you mean, 'Does she act?',"
said Ms Wiz. "The answer is, 'Yes,
brilliantly'."

"Saved!" cried Dulcima. "Here are
your lines." She gave Caroline a
script. "Are you a quick learner?"

Caroline gulped. "Er, quite," she
said nervously.

"The part you play is of a scruffy
little chimney-sweep girl who turns
out to be the Duchess of Portland,"
said Nigel. "Just be yourself,
darling."

"We're on in five minutes," said
Dulcima, grabbing Caroline's hand.

"I'll take you to make-up and we can learn the lines together."

"Why's Caroline all dirty?" asked Little Musha a few minutes later, as she and Ms Wiz watched Heritage on a small television in the Green Room.

"Ssshhh!" said Ms Wiz, sitting nervously on the edge of her seat. "I think she's the best chimney-sweep I've ever seen on television."

At that moment, the camera closed in dramatically upon Caroline's face. "You mean," she said, as tears welled up in her eyes. "You mean that I'm your *daughter*?"

"Welcome, home," said Dulcima with a dazzling smile.

As Nigel, Dulcima and Caroline embraced, the theme music for Heritage swelled up behind them.

"Did Caroline do well?" asked
Little Musha.

"She was astonishing," said Ms
Wiz, dabbing her eyes.

Moments later, the door to the
Green Room was flung open and
the three actors entered.

"A star is born!" announced
Dulcima. "Caroline, you were
wonderful, darling. Wasn't she
wonderful, Nigel?"

"Lovely perf," said Nigel, adding
with a hint of sulkiness, " I didn't
think I was bad either."

"You were wonderful too," said
Caroline.

Ms Wiz looked at a nearby clock.
"Never mind the 'wonderful
darlings'," she said. "If we don't
hurry, your parents will be returning
to an empty house."

"What about my clothes?" asked
Caroline.

"Here they are," said Ms Wiz. "There's no time to take the soot off your face."

Caroline wriggled out of her clothes. "Bye, Nigel and Dulcie," she said breathlessly. "That was definitely the best fun I've ever had."

"Cheery-bye, darling," said Nigel.

Dulcima gave Caroline a kiss. "Will we be able to work together again soon?" she asked.

"I hope so," said Caroline.


Ms Wiz, Caroline and Little Musha ran as fast as they could down a long corridor.

"What about Herbert?" gasped Musha.

"I thought you didn't like rats," said Caroline.

"Poor Herbert! Left alone in television land."

"Don't worry," shouted Ms Wiz. "I've got him."

They ran up the stairs and through a trapdoor at the top.

"Home!" said Little Musha as, once again, they stood on top of the Smiths' television set. Just then, they all heard the sound of a key turning in the front door.

"Quick, Ms Wiz!" said Caroline. "Get us back to our normal size before my parents come in."

There was a humming noise from

the direction of Ms Wiz, and the next thing Caroline and Little Musha knew, they had fallen in a heap on the living-room floor. Everything in the room appeared to be back to normal.

"Well," said Mrs Smith, looking at the tangle of bodies on the floor. "Still up at eleven o'clock? I don't call that very good babysitting."

"We couldn't sleep," said Caroline. "I thought that, because tomorrow's

Saturday, it wouldn't matter too much."

"It doesn't," said Mr Smith, putting his arm around his wife's waist. "We've had a good time, so why shouldn't you?"

"Caroline," said Mrs Smith. "Your face is absolutely filthy. What have you been doing?"

Just then, the telephone rang. Mr and Mrs Smith looked at one another in surprise.

"Hullo," said Mrs Smith into the phone. "Yes . . . brilliant, I see. Could you call tomorrow after I've discussed it with her and her father?"

"Who was it?" asked Mr Smith.

"It was a television producer," said Mrs Smith, looking puzzled. "He told me he thought Caroline was so good in something called Heritage, he wanted her to act in other programmes."

"Perhaps you ought to tell them

about it, Ms Wiz," smiled Caroline.

"Ms Wiz!" gasped Little Musha.
"You're getting *smaller*!"

"Oh no!" said Caroline. "Don't
leave me to explain it all."

Ms Wiz winked. "Whenever
magic's needed, I'll be back," she
said, smiling at Caroline. "Magic –
and fun."

"I can't believe my eyes," said Mr
Smith.

"She's really tiny now," said Little
Musha. There was a little pop, like a
bubble bursting, and Ms Wiz had
disappeared.

For a moment, the Smith family
stood in silence.

"Could you kindly tell us what's
been going on?" said Mrs Smith
finally.

"It's a long story," said Caroline.
"And I think you had better sit down
first."

# MS WIZ
# BANNED

# CHAPTER ONE

# A Friend In Need Is A Friend Indeed

Just because you can do a few magic spells, and fly, and turn people into animals now and then, it doesn't make life any easier. Sometimes being a Paranormal Operative can be really hard work.

"Yes," said Ms Wiz, putting the telephone on to boil. "Being magical is no bowl of cherries, that's for sure."

She was in her flat and had a tough day ahead of her, doing her homework, learning new spells and revising the old ones.

Then there was the housework. Ms Wiz looked at the list of things to do which she had pasted on a notice-board in her kitchen. It read:

1. Tell the vacuum cleaner to do the bedroom.
2. Put a washing and ironing spell on a dirty pile of clothes.
3. Speak roughly to the duster about the book shelves which haven't been touched for weeks.

"Flats don't clean themselves, you know," she said to Herbert, the magic rat, who was asleep in the corner.

"You can help me by cleaning out your cage right now."

Herbert twitched his nose and went back to sleep.

"Just a quick cup of tea," Ms Wiz said to herself. "Then I'll get on with those spells." She glanced at the telephone and sighed. It was true what people said – a watched telephone never boils. Just then the teapot rang.

"Hullo," said Ms Wiz, picking up the lid.

"Er, you won't remember me," said a man's voice from the teapot. "But I'm a school inspector. We met once at St Barnabas School."

Ms Wiz smiled. The last time she had seen the School Inspector, he had been running across the playground without his trousers on after Herbert the rat had run up his left leg.

"Of course I remember you," she said.

"We have a bit of a crisis here," said the School Inspector. "I wouldn't have called you but you're my last hope. We need your help."

"Tell me about the crisis," said Ms Wiz.

"Well," said the School Inspector, "it all began at yesterday's morning assembly . . ."

*

130

It had all begun at yesterday's morning assembly.

The highlight of assembly at St Barnabas was when the Head Teacher Mr Gilbert spoke about his Thought for the Day. This lasted for five (or, if it was a particularly big Thought, for ten) minutes and could be about any important subject.

One day the Thought might be "A Friend in Need is a Friend Indeed." Or "Great Oaks from Little Acorns Grow." Or "Neighbours, Everybody Needs Good Neighbours."

The children of Class Three liked Mr Gilbert's Thought for the Day. It gave Katrina the chance to finish the homework she should have done the previous evening. Her friend Podge used those few minutes to eat a couple of chocolate biscuits he had brought in his pocket. And Podge's friend Jack, who always went to bed too late, could catch up on some sleep.

But yesterday, the day of the crisis, Mr Gilbert's Thought had been most unusual.

"I think," he said, "I think I'm going to be sick."

Because so many of the children were busy doing their homework, or eating, or sleeping, no one paid much attention. But then Mr Gilbert sat down heavily on one of several empty chairs in the front row.

At that moment, Miss Peters leapt to her feet and said quickly, "Now, children, until Mr Gilbert feels better, we'll sing our favourite song, 'Lord of the Dance'." She sat down at the piano and, with a brave smile, began to sing "Dance, dance, wherever you may be."

"He won't be doing much dancing," whispered Katrina to

Podge, as the Head Teacher tottered down the aisle and out of the door. "Who's going to run the school now? Miss Gomaz, Mrs Hicks and Mr Williams are all ill too."

"Perhaps we'll all be sent home," said Podge when he had finished his biscuit.

". . . Otherwise they'll all have to be sent home," the School Inspector said to Ms Wiz the next day. "We need someone to run the school for a week. We're desperate."

"You want me to be the head of St Barnabas?" Ms Wiz could hardly believe her ears.

"And we need other teachers too," said the School Inspector.

"Leave it to me," said Ms Wiz. "Your crisis is over."

"And, er, Ms Wiz." The School

Inspector sounded embarrassed.

"May I make one small request?"

"Of course."

"Go easy on the magic, all right?"

Ms Wiz sighed. Why *was* it that people were so nervous about a few spells these days?

"Trust me," she said.

At the next morning's assembly, the children of St Barnabas noticed that there was a stranger sitting in the Head Teacher's chair. She wore a dark suit, a black gown and had a funny square hat on her head.

"She doesn't look much fun," Caroline whispered to Katrina.

"Come back Mr Gilbert, all is forgiven," said Katrina.

The woman stood up and said quietly, "Good morning, children. My name is Miss Wyzbrovicz. I'm

Mr Gilbert's replacement. I'd like to introduce you to my two assistants who are here to help me this week."

From the front row, a small, neat woman in glasses and an older, grey-haired man stepped forward and stood on each side of her.

The new Head Teacher took off her hat, and shook her head, allowing long dark hair to fall on her shoulders. Then she started clicking her fingers. "One, two, three, four," she said.

To the astonishment of everyone in assembly, the woman's two assistants started clapping their hands in time.

"What on earth?" muttered Jack who, for the first time in living memory, was awake during assembly.

Suddenly the Head Teacher began to talk – or rather to sing.

*"Morning, everybody, get into that beat,
Listen to me, children, and tap those
   feet."*

"I don't believe it," said Katrina.

"The Head Teacher's doing a song," said Podge.

*"It's morning assembly and your feet's a-tappin'*

*As you hear your new Head Teacher a-rappin'."*

Now the grey-haired man joined in, singing,

*"My name's Mr Warlock, now listen to me,*

*I'm here to teach ya some geographee."*

"A rap song?" said Jack, his jaw sagging. "At St Barnabas morning assembly?"

The other teacher stepped forward.
*"I'm Miss N Chanter but don't be*
    *afraid*
*I'll show you how magic potions are*
    *made."*

"Magic potions!" Caroline smiled. "That must be it. When things get this strange, there can only be one person behind it."

"Of course," said Podge. "Look at the black nail varnish on the Head Teacher's hands."

Soon the whole of Class Three were clapping in time to the song.

The Head Teacher smiled, pointed the fingers of both hands at the children and sang,
    *"So, kids, I'm here to teach you the biz*
    *You know me, my name's—"*

"Ms Wiz!" shouted everyone in Class Three.

Outside the School Hall, the School Inspector listened. He had a busy day ahead, but was just calling by to see that the new Head Teacher was settling in all right. From the sounds coming from assembly, she seemed to be getting on well, even if it was a bit noisy.

"Phew," he said, glancing at his watch. "At least there's no magic around."

# CHAPTER TWO

# Travel Broadens The Mind

No magic?

The children of Class Three who clustered around Ms Wiz after assembly were shocked by the news she brought them.

"What about Herbert the rat?" asked Caroline.

"And flying around the classroom on your vacuum cleaner?" asked Katrina.

"And turning teachers into warthogs?" asked Jack.

Ms Wiz held up her hands for silence.

"The School Inspector has invited me to St Barnabas on condition that there's no magic," she said.

The children groaned.

"Why?" asked Katrina.

"Because spells make grown-ups nervous, that's why," said Ms Wiz, putting on her square hat. "So I'm going to be a serious Head Teacher."

"Who's in charge of Class Three this week?" asked Caroline. "Mr Williams is off sick."

"I've given you Mr Warlock," said Ms Wiz. "I think you'll find him very interesting, but this is his first teaching job. Can I depend on you to be nice to him?"

"You can depend on us," said Jack. "We're Class Three."

"That's what worries me," said Ms Wiz.


"Is it true that you're a wizard, sir?"

"Jack!" hissed Caroline.
"Remember what Ms Wiz said."

Mr Warlock stood at the door of the

classroom and stared in amazement at Class Three.

"Excuse me for asking," Jack continued, ignoring Caroline. "It's just that I've got a book at home called *Witches, Warlocks and Other Weird Creatures*."

Katrina put up her hand. "And the other new teacher's called Miss N Chanter," she said.

"Nicola Chanter, yes," said Mr Warlock.

"N Chanter. That means that she *enchants*, doesn't it?"

Mr Warlock took off his glasses, laid them on the desk and looked at Class Three very seriously.

"I don't know what you're talking about," he said. "I'm just as normal as any other teacher."

"Which isn't very normal," murmured Jack.

"All right," said the new teacher. "Answer your names, please." He read

out the register. There was only one person missing and that was Carl, the youngest boy in the class.

"Carl's always late," said Lizzie. "He probably thinks it's a Saturday."

The teacher frowned and made a note of Carl's name.

"Now today we're going to do some geography," he said, unrolling a map of the world that he had brought with him and pinning it on to the blackboard. "Who likes geography?"

There was silence from Class Three.

"Learning map signs," muttered Podge. "Discovering the difference between an isthmus and a peninsula. That's really interesting, isn't it?"

Mr Warlock looked surprised.

"Well," he said, reaching into his briefcase, "I think you'll like it after today."

144

He laid a box on his desk and took out three darts.

"Who knows the capital city of Norway?" he asked.

Caroline put up her hand.

"Oslo," she said.

Mr Warlock gave her a dart.

"And the highest mountain in the world?"

Jack put up his hand.

"Mount Everest," he said.

Mr Warlock gave him a dart.

"And who can give me the name of a major European city where there are no pedestrian crossings?"

There was silence. Mr Warlock smiled and put up his hand.

"Venice," he said. "Because all the streets are canals." He gave himself a dart. "Well done, Mr Warlock," he said.

"This is a *normal* teacher?" muttered Jack under his breath.

"Now, the two children with darts should come to the front of the class and throw them at the map," said Mr Warlock.

Caroline went to the front and threw her dart. Then Jack did the same. The teacher was about to throw his dart when Katrina asked, "What's this got to do with geography, sir?"

Mr Warlock looked surprised.

"Didn't I tell you?" he said. "I'm

taking you on a field trip to the most interesting place one of the darts lands on."

Caroline looked at where her dart had stuck in the map.

"Mine's in Milton Keynes," she said. "And Jack's is in the middle of the Atlantic Ocean."

"Oh dear, that's not very interesting," said Mr Warlock. He threw his dart, which made an odd humming noise as it flew through the air.

"Where did it land, Caroline?" he asked.

Caroline looked closely at the map.

"On a small island called Sombrero," she said. "It's in the Caribbean Ocean."

Mr Warlock smiled. "That's more like it," he said.

"I still don't see what's wrong with

Milton Keynes," muttered Podge, but no one was listening.

It wasn't that Carl meant to be late for everything. It was just that things were always happening to him that didn't happen to other people.

On this particular morning, for example, a cat followed him down the street. Since he was going towards a main road, he had to take the cat back to where he had first seen it. But then the cat followed him again. He took it back. On his third trip, carrying the cat back, its owner came out of the house and thought Carl was trying to steal it. It took quite a long time to explain the problem, by which time Carl was late for school yet again.

Nervously, he knocked on the Head Teacher's door.

"Come in," said a voice from inside.

Carl was surprised to find a woman sitting at Mr Gilbert's desk. She was playing chess with a rat.

"I was looking for Mr Gilbert," he said.

The woman smiled. "I'm Head Teacher this week," she said. "You can call me Ms Wiz."

"Ms Wiz!" said Carl, who had only

come to St Barnabas that term. "I've heard about you. You're the person who appears whenever a bit of magic's needed, aren't you?"

"That's right," said Ms Wiz. "Now what's the problem?"

Carl took some time to explain why he was late for school.

"I went to my classroom but no one seems to be there," he said.

"Really?" Ms Wiz looked concerned.

"All I could find was a notice on the blackboard," Carl said. "It read, 'GONE ON A FIELD TRIP TO THE SUNNY TROPICAL ISLAND OF SOMBRERO – BACK SOON!' What could that mean?"

"I think," said Ms Wiz, who had gone quite pale, "that it means I'm in dead trouble."

# CHAPTER THREE

# Ask No Questions, Hear No Lies

"I *knew* it," said Ms Wiz, as she hurried across the playground with Carl running behind her. "I knew those two would start casting spells as soon as my back was turned."

"Which two?" Carl asked.

"Mr Warlock and Miss N Chanter," said Ms Wiz. "They're both Paranormal Operatives. Magic is as natural to them as flying."

As *flying*? Carl frowned. "But why didn't you just tell them to be normal?" he asked. "After all, you are Head Teacher. They're supposed to be able to boss people around."

Ms Wiz groaned. "I'm just not the bossing kind, I suppose," she muttered.

151

When they arrived at Class Three's empty room, Ms Wiz went straight to the map on the blackboard and pulled out three darts that were sticking into it.

"Oh no," she said. "Warlock's been using his magic darts again – and he's left them behind. Heaven knows how he'll get Class Three back here again."

Carl was looking at Class Three's lockers. "They won't be here for lunch anyway," he said. "They've taken their lunchboxes."

Ms Wiz sighed. "We'd better go and see Class Four," she said. "I don't trust Miss Chanter either."

As they entered the classroom next door, Carl couldn't help noticing that there was an unusual number of pet rabbits hopping about the room.

"Wow," he said. "I never knew Class Four kept rabbits."

Miss Chanter smiled and looked around the room.

"The class don't keep rabbits," she explained. "They *are* rabbits. If they can't spell properly, I'm turning them into—"

"No no *no*!" shouted Ms Wiz suddenly. "No magic, no spells, no rabbits, no potions, no broomsticks! I've already lost Class Three to a sunny tropical island. Turn these rabbits back into children immediately."

Grumbling, Miss N Chanter uttered a spell. Before Carl's astonished eyes, the rabbits became children once more.

"That's better," said Ms Wiz. "From now on, Miss Chanter, it's the three R's for Class Four. Reading, writing and—"

"Rabbiting about?" suggested Jamie, a small red-haired boy sitting at the back of the class.

"No," said Ms Wiz. "Responsibility. I expect you all to be responsible while I try to get your friends in Class Three back from the other side of the world."

"Well, really," said Miss N Chanter, after Ms Wiz and Carl had left the room. "She used to be such fun before she was Head Teacher."

"It's always the same," said Jamie. "Class Three get the excitement and we get the telling off."

"Yeah." The rest of the class joined in. "It's really unfair, Miss."

The teacher scratched her head thoughtfully. "Perhaps I could take you on a trip around town," she said.

"We've seen the town," said Mary, who was sitting beside Jamie. "We live here."

"Yes," said Miss N Chanter. "But have you seen it from the sky?"

*

Ms Wiz had the nastiest surprise
imaginable when she returned
to the office with Carl. The School
Inspector was waiting for her.

"Good morning to you, Ms Wiz,"
he smiled. "I was just passing by and
I thought I'd look in to see how you
were getting on."

"Er, quite well, thank you," said Ms
Wiz nervously. "Everything's going
swimmingly."

"And who's our young friend
here?" the School Inspector asked,
nodding in Carl's direction.

"He's in Class Three with Mr
Warlock," said Ms Wiz.

"They've gone on a field trip," said
Carl quickly.

The School Inspector nodded.
"Where to?" he asked.

Ms Wiz had turned quite pale. Then
she straightened her back and said,
"I cannot tell a lie. Mr Warlock

appears to have taken them to Sombrero."

"And where precisely is Sombrero?"

There was another silence, during which the clock in Mr Gilbert's office could be heard ticking.

"It's a small island in the Caribbean," said Ms Wiz weakly.

It was at this moment that Carl saw something out of the office window which attracted his attention. Miss N Chanter was opening a door and a flock of pigeons was following her into the sunlight. One of them was the same colour red as Jamie's hair.

"Are you telling me that an entire class has disappeared to the other side of the world?" There was a faint hint of panic in the School Inspector's voice. "Am I to understand that there has been magic on these premises in spite of my specific instructions?"

Ms Wiz nodded miserably.

The School Inspector leapt to his feet.

"Right, that's it," he cried. "Rats up trouser legs are one thing – disappearing children are quite another. I'm calling the police and then I'm going to the Town Hall. I'll get you banned for life! Now, please pack your things and go. You will not be allowed back on the premises."

"But, sir," said Carl. "How are you going to get Class Three back if you ban Ms Wiz?"

The School Inspector looked at Carl as if he were about to swat him like a fly.

"There are such things as aeroplanes," he said nastily.

After he had left, Ms Wiz slumped into her chair.

"I should never have agreed to be a Head Teacher," she groaned. "Magic and a sense of responsibility don't seem to go together."

"Oh well," said Carl, anxious to cheer her up. "At least he didn't see the pigeons."

"Pigeons? Did you say pigeons?"

"They just walked out of Class Four's door and flew off," said Carl.

Ms Wiz had buried her face in her hands and was making an odd moaning sound.

"Let's just hope they're homing pigeons," said Carl.

The sun shone brightly on the lovely tropical island of Sombrero. The waves of the bright blue Caribbean lapped softly on the white sand and a gentle breeze carried the sound of calypso guitar across the beach. It was certainly the best field trip that Class Three had ever been on.

Katrina and Caroline sat under a palm tree, listening to a man playing a guitar, fanning themselves with their exercise books. Jack had found a skateboard ramp nearby and was showing the local children some tricks. Podge had cracked open a coconut and was using the top of his pen as a spoon. Lizzie was collecting seashells, and the rest of the class were paddling in the waves.

"Anyone got the time?" asked Mr

Warlock, sleepily sipping an orange drink through a straw. "We must remember to get back home before tea-time."

"Haven't you even got a watch?" said Lizzie, as she inspected a starfish.

"Must have left it at home in my case," said Mr Warlock. "It's probably with the magic darts."

"So how are we going to get home then?" asked Lizzie.

"That's just what I was wondering," yawned Mr Warlock sleepily. "I expect Ms Wiz knows the spell."

# CHAPTER FOUR

# Look Before You Leap

One of Mr Gilbert's favourite Thoughts for the Day was "When One Door Closes, Another One Opens." If Ms Wiz had been asked for her Thought this particular day, it might have been "When One Door Closes, The Ceiling Falls Down On Your Head." Or ... "Just When You Think Things Can't Get Worse, They Do." Or ... "Help, Get Me Out Of Here!"

Class Three had disappeared to the other side of the world.

Class Four had taken wing and were flying around in the clouds.

The School Inspector was reporting her to the police and was about to get her banned from the school.

"The important thing is not to panic," said Carl, as they sat in the Head Teacher's study, wondering what to do next.

"Yes, good, absolutely right," said Ms Wiz, panicking.

"If we can just get the two classes back by the end of the day," said Carl, "we can pretend that the School Inspector invented it all."

Ms Wiz sat up straight in her chair and looked at him sternly.

"I cannot tell a lie," she said.

"Of course not," said Carl. "Anyway, you're magic. I'm sure you can do it."

Ms Wiz sighed. "But I don't know the travelling spell," she said.

"Oh dear," said Carl gloomily.

"Of course, Miss N Chanter knows it but she's too busy being a pigeon to be much use."

"Oh dear, oh dear," said Carl even more gloomily.

Ms Wiz stood up suddenly, picked up her chair and walked towards the door.

"We'll just have to go and get help," she said. "Bring your chair to the playground, will you, Carl?"

"My *chair*?" Bewildered, Carl followed her out of the room, carrying his chair.

Moments later, amid a loud humming noise, Carl and Ms Wiz were hovering a few feet above the playground.

"Flying chairs!" Carl gasped. "Don't we need seat belts?"

"Of course not," smiled Ms Wiz. "This is magic."

The chairs rose high above the school, turned slowly towards the east and rose into the clouds.

"Where are we going?" Carl shouted above the sound of the wind whistling past his ears.

"Headquarters," said Ms Wiz.

Headquarters? Carl remembered Lizzie saying that she had seen Ms Wiz's home, an old car, when she had helped rescue Lizzie's cat from burglars, but no one had ever mentioned headquarters.

"Is it far?" he asked.

"Beyond Ongar," said Ms Wiz.

Beyond Ongar! Carl had never heard of Ongar, let alone a place beyond it.

Soon the chairs were descending rapidly through the clouds, coming to rest in a quiet back street in front of a tall office block with dark windows. By the entrance, there was a sign which read "PO HEADQUARTERS".

"Here we are," said Ms Wiz, jumping off her chair. "The headquarters of the Paranormal Operatives."

"I always thought PO stood for Post Office," said Carl.

"So do a lot of people," said Ms Wiz with a smile. "They keep sending their parcels here."

"That explains why the post is always late," Carl muttered as he followed Ms Wiz through some glass doors and into the building.

At first he thought that the office reception area was like any other. Then he noticed that all the people working there had black nail varnish. And that there was a sign on the wall which said "REMEMBER! WE ARE NOT WITCHES! WE ARE PARANORMAL OPERATIVES." And that a secretary nearby was reading a book called *Notions for Potions – Some Paranormal Recipes* while the keyboard beside her worked itself.

Ms Wiz walked up to the reception desk.

"I have urgent business with the travel department," she told the receptionist.

"Would that be time travel, space travel, inter-continental travel, inter-galactic travel, underwater travel, mind travel or holiday bookings?" the woman asked, filing one of her black fingernails.

"I need to get some children back from the other side of the world," said Ms Wiz.

"That'll be inter-continental travel," said the receptionist sleepily. "Mr Broom, our inter-continental travel executive, has gone for lunch in the Seychelles."

"Then get him back," said Ms Wiz sharply.

"I don't have the spell, do I?" said the woman.

"Who has got it?" asked Carl, thinking that at this rate they would never get Class Three back by the end of the day.

The woman looked at him coldly.

"Mr Broom," she said. "And he's gone for—"

"Enough!" Ms Wiz slammed the desk. "If you don't want to spend the rest of the day as a toad, you'll get him right now."

The woman shrugged. "Room 305 on the third floor," she said. "I'll see what I can do."

When Ms Wiz and Carl reached Room 305, they found a young man wearing a bathing suit and dark glasses sitting behind the desk.

"This had better be important," he said moodily. "I was just going for a swim in the sea when I was called back."

"It is," said Ms Wiz. "It's a case of missing children."

Mr Broom frowned as Ms Wiz explained the situation. Then he turned to a computer beside his desk and tapped some keys on the keyboard. Within seconds, a tropical scene appeared on the screen.

"There appears to be some sort of beach party going on," said Mr Broom. "Can you see any of your friends, young man?"

Carl moved nearer to the screen. "There's Podge at the barbecue," he said suddenly. "And Katrina's dancing by the radio. Mr Warlock seems to be asleep under a tree."

"Are you sure you want to get them back?" asked Mr Broom. "They seem to be having a very good time."

"Absolutely," said Ms Wiz. "All good things come to an end."

"Well, first of all you have to get the magic darts," said Mr Broom.

"But they're at St Barnabas," said Ms Wiz. "And I'm not allowed back."

Mr Broom shrugged. "Then you'll just have to find someone to work the spell for you," he said.

And suddenly Ms Wiz was smiling at Carl.

# CHAPTER FIVE

# Small Is Beautiful

There were times when Carl wished that he wasn't late for everything, and that afternoon, as he walked through the gates of St Barnabas carrying a pencil case, was one of them. If it hadn't been for the cat following him this morning, he would be with Class Three now, enjoying the sun and sand of Sombrero.

Instead he was the only person in the world who could bring them back and save Ms Wiz from getting into more trouble. He was going to cast a spell, like a real Paranormal Operative. It was a bit dangerous, Ms Wiz had said, but she trusted him.

As far as Carl could remember, this was the first time that anyone had ever trusted him with anything.

The School Inspector was pacing up and down inside the school gates like a watchdog.

"What are you doing, young man?" he asked suspiciously.

Carl held up the pencil case that Mr Broom at PO Headquarters had given him.

"I forgot my pencil case," he said. "I went home to fetch it."

The School Inspector did not look entirely convinced. "You haven't seen that Ms Wiz woman, have you?" he asked. "She seems to have vanished into thin air."

"That's because you banned her," said Carl.

"Hmm," said the School Inspector. "Just as long as she's not lurking about somewhere."

Inside the pencil case, Ms Wiz clung on to a fountain pen for dear life. She had agreed to help Carl with the travelling spell by making herself small enough to be smuggled into school.

From inside the case, she heard Carl telling the School Inspector that he had to fetch his books from Class Three's room so that he could work in the library. The pencil case shook as he ran across the playground.

Once again Ms Wiz gripped the fountain pen.

"The things I do for magic," she sighed.

As soon as they were in the classroom, Carl opened the case and carefully lifted Ms Wiz on to the desk.

"There's no time to lose," she said. "Grab the darts and I'll tell you the spell you've got to say."

"*I've* got to say?"

"I thought you wanted to see Sombrero," said Ms Wiz.

"I do, but—"

"Fine," smiled Ms Wiz. "You've got half an hour to travel across the world and bring your friends back. It's a piece of cake."

"What will you do while I'm away?" Carl asked.

"I suppose I'll have to hide in this case," said Ms Wiz. "The School

Inspector seems to be looking out for me."

"I won't be long," said Carl, holding the darts tightly in his hand. Repeating the words after Ms Wiz, he muttered the spell. Suddenly there was a humming noise and, for a few seconds, Carl felt like an arrow flying through the air, buffeted by the wind. He squeezed his eyes shut until the shaking stopped. Then he heard voices.

"Hey, it's Carl."

"What's he doing here?"

"Late as usual."

"Wake up, Carl. You're just in time for the limbo competition."

Slowly Carl opened his eyes. It was warm. The sunlight was dazzling. He could hear the distant sound of waves. And, all around him, were the children of Class Three.

"Phew," said Carl, dusting himself down. "I made it."

"Come and do the limbo," said Katrina. "You have to lean back and dance under this low pole. It's great."

Carl looked doubtful. "We haven't got much time before we have to get back," he said.

"Carl worrying about the time," Jack laughed. "I've heard everything now."

"All right," said Carl. "Someone go and wake up Mr Warlock. I'll have a

quick limbo and then we'll be on
our way."

Back at St Barnabas, Ms Wiz sat in the
darkness of Mr Broom's pencil case
and thought about the past.

She remembered her adventures
with the children of Class Three – the
prizegiving when Mr Gilbert was
turned into a sheep, the time when a

local hospital was invaded by white mice, the hunt for Lizzie's stolen cat, the day when Jack let loose ghosts and demons in a library, her adventures in a television set with Caroline and Little Musha.

"I've certainly been there whenever magic was needed," she said to herself. "But maybe it's time to move to another school. Or even to another country."

She paced up and down in the darkness. Carl had been gone almost ten minutes now. What if the spell had sent him to the wrong place? Or he couldn't remember how to get back? Or he had lost the magic darts? If something happened to her friends, she would never forgive herself.

But then Ms Wiz smiled. Outside the pencil case, she heard a distant hum which grew louder and louder. Suddenly the classroom was alive with the sound of children's voices.

"Wow," Podge was saying. "I've just had the weirdest dream. I thought I was on a tropical island."

"That was no dream," Carl said. Ms Wiz felt the pencil case being lifted, its top opened slowly. She looked up and saw familiar faces looking down at her. "That was Wizardry," Carl smiled.

Ms Wiz climbed out of the pencil case and stood on the desk. It was difficult behaving like a serious Head Teacher when you were only three inches tall, but she had to give it a try.

"Now where's Mr Warlock?" she asked.

"He wanted to go straight home," said Carl. "So I gave him the spell and the second dart."

"I think he was embarrassed at being unable to get us back," said Lizzie.

"Quite right too," said Ms Wiz. "Now, since I've been banned from the school, Carl is going to have to smuggle me out."

"What happens if the School Inspector asks where we've been?" asked Jack.

Ms Wiz straightened her back and looked at him sternly. "You should say, 'I cannot tell a—' "

"I think we should lie," said Carl firmly. "Just this once."

"All right," said Ms Wiz. "Say you went to a museum."

At that moment, there was a loud thudding noise on the roof of the classroom.

"That will be Class Four," smiled Ms Wiz. "Miss N Chanter's very punctual. Can they get down all right?"

"There's a ladder leading down from the roof," said Katrina.

"Good," said Ms Wiz, as a pigeon appeared at the window, hovered for a moment and then flew off. "Miss Chanter's off home." She glanced at a clock on the wall. "It's time for you all to go too. Your parents will be waiting for you."

"When will we see you again?" asked Podge.

"Well, right now I'm going to take a holiday," said Ms Wiz, reaching inside the pencil case and pulling out some bright yellow trousers. "I've even brought my holiday clothes."

"But you'll be back, won't you?" asked Caroline. "Whenever magic's needed?"

Ms Wiz paused as she climbed back into the case. "I hope so," she said with a smile, before closing the lid over her head.

Carl walked home slowly. Just once he looked inside the case. There, in the corner, was the tiny black dress of a head teacher.

Carefully putting it into his jacket pocket, Carl went over the strange, magical events of the day, wondering whether he would ever see his paranormal friend again. He smiled at the thought of her.

" 'Bye, Ms Wiz," he said quietly.